FRENCH DUCKS in VENICE

For Max and Maizie Newman, my favorite ducks

G. F. W.

For my mom, for everything, and Drew, for everything else

E. M.

Text copyright © 2011 by Garret Freymann-Weyr
Illustrations copyright © 2011 by Erin McGuire

First edition 2011

Library of Congress Cataloging-in-Publication Data

Freymann-Weyr, Garret, date.
French ducks in Venice / Garret Freymann-Weyr ; illustrated by Erin McGuire.
— 1st ed.
p. cm.
Summary: When Polina Panova's "prince" moves out of their Venice, California, house,
two ducks that live on the canals but believe themselves to be French try to help Polina, a designer
of magical dresses of thread, silk, velvet, grass, and pieces of night sky, by giving
her something to make her stop being sad.
ISBN 978-0-7636-4173-3
[1. Ducks—Fiction. 2. Canals—Fiction. 3. Venice (Calif.)—Fiction.]
I. McGuire, Erin, ill. II. Title.
PZ7.F893Fr 2011
[Fic]—dc22   2010047672

11 12 13 14 15 16 SCP 10 9 8 7 6 5 4 3 2 1

Printed in Humen, Dongguan, China

This book was typeset in Filosofia.
The illustrations were created digitally.

Candlewick Press
99 Dover Street
Somerville, Massachusetts 02144

visit us at www.candlewick.com

FRENCH DUCKS
in VENICE

Garret Freymann-Weyr
ILLUSTRATED BY Erin McGuire

CANDLEWICK PRESS

The Venice in this story is not the one in Italy, full of gondolas, churches, and pigeons. Instead, our Venice is the one in California, full of surfers, bungalows, and seagulls.

And our ducks, it should be said, are not French. They may not even be ducks, although I would advise against telling them that.

What is certain is that they are small birds with glossy black feathers, white tails, long necks, and yellow beaks. They swim and eat all the green gunky things that grow underwater. They think of themselves as ducks. And as French. No one knows why (not even the ducks themselves), but that's how it is.

The other ducks on the canal where the French ducks live think of them as odd.

Georges and his sister, Cécile, don't mind. They think of the other ducks as ordinary.

"Mallards," Georges says with a sniff.

"Such green necks," Cécile says. "Such brown feathers."

The other ducks are not important. They may gossip about their unusual neighbors, but they play no other role in our story.

Georges and Cécile do have an important friend, however. Her name is Polina Panova, and she is not a duck. Or French.

She is Russian, and our French ducks think she is a princess.

Polina thinks this is very funny.

"Princess of what?" Polina always asks them. "I live in a house on the canal. I make dresses. Hardly a princess."

"Only a princess could make such beautiful dresses," Georges has told her.

He could say this with confidence, because every now and then, Georges and Cécile are allowed to visit with Polina in her house. The house on the canal is both where she lives and where she sews her dresses. The dresses are beautiful enough to admire even if you do not wear dresses, or, for that matter, any kind of clothes.

"How do you make them?" Georges asks one day when he and Cécile are allowed to visit.

He knows the answer, of course, but he likes to look at the dresses while Polina talks about them.

"I make the dresses with thread, silk, cotton, and velvet," Polina says. "Also grass, flowers, pieces of the night sky, and strawberry jam."

Women and girls come from across the world to buy them. They do not know about the flowers, or the night sky, or the jam. What they *do* know is that when you wear a dress made by Polina Panova, anything can happen.

A cat might follow you home and demand to come in for a cup of tea. Or a tree might ask you to dance. Or you may simply go to school and have one of those really good days. The kind where you know the answers to all your questions and and no one is in a bad mood.

"It's true that the dresses are special," Polina says with a proud smile. "But that doesn't make me a princess; it only makes me clever."

"Only a princess could live with a prince," Cécile says.

Sebastian Sterling lives with Polina in her house on the canal. Sebastian is not French or Russian, but he is very obviously a prince. He is tall and handsome, with a perfect nose, blue eyes, and strong shoulders. However, the ducks know it's not his looks that make Sebastian a prince.

It's what he does.

Every morning, a huge black car comes to pick up Sebastian. The car swoops down the hills away from Venice and toward the studios in Los Angeles.

Sebastian Sterling makes movies. Movies made of shadows, silver, and a light so shimmering that it almost hurts your eyes to look at it. People across the world line up at theaters to watch his movies. Sebastian Sterling's movies make people happy and peaceful and amazed.

The ducks know that whenever Polina looks at Sebastian, she is happy and peaceful and amazed.

"I suppose you are right," Polina says later. "He is a prince. Maybe that makes me a princess."

"Don't forget the dresses," Georges says.

"Yes, don't forget about them," Cécile says.

Polina smiles. She loves the ducks, and likes to sit on one of the docks along the edge of the canal to enjoy her afternoon coffee. That way she can talk to them. French ducks are, by far, the best sort of ducks for coffee and conversation.

"Good-bye," she says when her coffee is done. "I will see you tomorrow."

"Good-bye," says Georges.

"Tomorrow," says Cécile. "We will see you tomorrow."

THE NEXT MORNING, the front door of Polina Panova's house opens. Out steps Sebastian Sterling, carrying a huge, heavy suitcase tied shut with ropes. Georges, who is gliding toward the house, is the first one to see him. Now, Sebastian has gone away on trips before. After all, when people across the world line up at theaters to see your movies, you have to go and meet them. It's only polite.

On those trips where he meets the people who line up to see his movies—the ones he makes of shadows, silver, and light—Sebastian takes a small cloth bag. Not a huge, heavy suitcase so full of things that it is tied shut with ropes.

"Cécile, turn around!" Georges calls out. "Sebastian Sterling is leaving!"

Cécile, who has been gliding toward the other side of the canal, turns sharply at the sound of her brother's voice. She sees Sebastian walking away from Polina's house.

"Sebastian goes on many trips," she says sternly.

She is about to remind Georges that this is the quiet and peaceful

hour of the morning, but then she sees the huge and heavy suitcase. It is the kind of suitcase you pack when you are going away forever.

"Where is he going, I wonder?" Georges says, feeling cross and thinking very hard.

Georges is not actually that fond of Sebastian. He believes that Sebastian Sterling does not appreciate how lucky he is to have two French ducks living right outside his door. But Georges knows how much Polina loves Sebastian. When he takes his short trips to meet the people who watch his movies, she is always a little bit sad.

It would, therefore, *not do* for him to go away forever.

Georges scrambles over the edge of the canal and begins racing after Sebastian Sterling.

"You wait! Stop that!" Georges says, not caring that it is the quiet and peaceful hour of the morning. "Sebastian Sterling, you stop right this instant!"

But Sebastian keeps walking on, getting farther and farther away from Polina's house.

Georges takes a deep breath and stretches his delicate black wings. This is the thing about French ducks: they are strong and beautiful fliers who very rarely fly. Living in Venice, as they do, on the canal, where they have everything they need, flying is only for emergencies.

Georges soars up into the air, trying not to think about how fast he is going. He knows, as he lands right in front of Polina's prince, that this is an emergency.

"Sebastian Sterling," he says, "where are you going?"

Cécile has followed her brother, and she looks from Georges to Sebastian.

"*Why* are you going?" Cécile asks gently.

Sebastian puts down his huge and heavy suitcase and looks at the two French ducks.

"I have to go," he says.

"Where?" Georges asks, not impressed with this four-word answer.

"Why?" Cécile asks, thinking that *why* is far more important than *where*.

Sebastian stands there with his perfect nose, blue eyes, and strong shoulders. He sighs, and then he picks up his suitcase.

"I have to go," he says, and walks past Georges.

"Oh, dear," Cécile says.

"This is very wrong," Georges says. "We'll have to follow him."

"Are you sure?" Cécile asks, not at all sure they should.

"Yes, I am sure," Georges says. "It will *not do* for him to go."

The French ducks stretch their delicate black wings, soar up into the air, and follow Sebastian Sterling. They follow him as he walks down Riviera Avenue, across Market Street. And then without warning, the sky is filled with clouds. These are special clouds made of silver shadows and shimmering light, and their beauty almost hurts the French ducks' eyes. They keep flying. By the time they find their way out of the silver shadows and shimmering light, Sebastian Sterling has vanished.

Georges and Cécile fly near and far. They fly high and low. They swoop all along Venice and Santa Monica. They ask all the creatures who live on Riviera Avenue and Market Street, "Did you see which way Sebastian Sterling went?"

All the creatures say the same thing. They say, "He was here, walking. And then, just like that, with no warning, he was gone."

Georges and Cécile fly and search until their wings shake. It's time to go home. To the canal where Polina lives.

Alone.

That afternoon, Polina comes out carrying her coffee and sits down on the edge of the canal.

"Polina! Polina!" Georges calls out, swimming quickly over to her.

"Hello, Georges," Polina says.

"Sebastian Sterling has left," Georges says. "He's gone!"

"Yes, I know," Polina says. "He had to go."

"We tried to follow him," Georges says. "But he vanished."

"Georges, stop bothering Polina," Cécile says.

"But Sebastian Sterling has gone," Georges says. "Where? Why?"

"He had to go," Polina says a second time.

"He's gone away with the kind of suitcase you pack when you are going away forever," Georges says.

"That's how it is," Polina says, sadly but truthfully.

Georges starts to say something, but Cécile gives him a stern look. It is the kind of stern look which means, "Shush."

Polina says, "Try not to bother yourself, Georges."

But Georges is bothered.

Polina Panova is now a Russian princess without a prince.

"This will *not do*," he says to his sister, expecting her to agree.

But Cécile thinks it will do just fine.

"It will have to do," she says.

"But Sebastian Sterling is gone," Georges says. "And Polina is sad."

"It's true," Cécile says. "That's how it is."

Georges does not think much of how it is.

Instead of finding Sebastian Sterling, who had to go and is not to be found, Georges decides that he will find a present for Polina. A pretty, perfect present for his princess. It will mean that he must fly near and far, and high and low.

To gain strength, Georges rests and eats the greenest of the green gunky things that grow under the water. When he is ready, our French duck stretches his delicate black wings and flies off into the soft, inviting air of Venice.

When he reaches the ocean, he examines some glass beads, which the sea birds, who are not to be trusted, say are exquisite.

"No, thank you," Georges says, who does not trust a word with an x and a q in it.

Also, the glass beads remind him of the silver shadows and shimmering light in the special clouds that surrounded Sebastian Sterling when he vanished.

Georges flies on, looking high and low.

Perhaps a rope of salt and seaweed, suggests a dolphin, busy jumping in and out of the ocean.

"No, thank you," Georges says, because, after all, what would Polina do with a rope of salt and seaweed?

Also, the rope of salt and seaweed reminds him of the huge, heavy suitcase tied shut with ropes that Sebastian Sterling carried on the morning when he had to go.

Georges flies on, looking near and far. He is beginning to get tired when he spots, in the distance, a faint light that both shines and bounces. On he flies, full of hope, until he gets to where the sky meets the ocean.

This is not an easy place to find, and, once there, Georges is immediately surrounded by a golden, soothing light, with shining, bouncing bits inside of it. It is the kind of light that does not hurt your eyes.

The ocean roars its hello, and the sky swirls its greeting.

"Hello," Georges says politely, and then he explains about Polina Panova, who is sad, and Sebastian Sterling, who had to go.

"I need a present for my princess," Georges says. "It will *not do* for her to be sad."

The sky and the ocean know how much Georges loves Polina. They know how well he will look after her, and they think he is very brave to have come all this way. There is swirling and roaring as they consider his request.

"Well," says the sky. "You have had a long trip."

"Well," says the ocean. "You *do* need a perfect present."

Very carefully, they hand Georges a long piece of the golden, soothing light from where they meet. He wraps all of its shining, bouncing bits around his neck.

"Thank you," he says, wondering how in the world he will fly home with this present. The light from where the sky and ocean meet is as helpful as it is soothing, and it lifts Georges's delicate black wings. Together, they return to Venice and to Polina's house on the canal.

"My goodness," Cécile says, seeing all the bouncy, shining bits.

The two French ducks show the golden, soothing light how to pour itself under Polina's door and through her windows.

Cécile would like to ask Georges all about his journey, but instead she orders the mallards to be quiet and tucks her brother into bed.

He falls instantly asleep.

When he wakes up, it is well past the quiet and peaceful hour of the morning, and Polina is already sitting by the canal, drinking her afternoon coffee.

"Hello, Georges," she says. "Thank you for the present."

"Are you happy now?" he asks.

"I am happy to see you," Polina says.

"But you are still sad that Sebastian Sterling had to go," Georges says.

Polina nods, and Georges bows his head. There is nothing left for him to do.

That night Cécile tells her brother, "Polina has to be sad before she can be happy again."

"But she has no prince," Georges says. "How will she ever be happy again?"

"Maybe she will find a new prince," Cécile says. "When she is done being sad."

"When will she be done?" Georges asks.

"I don't know," Cécile says.

"I will start looking for her new prince," Georges says. "For when she is happy again."

"Ducks do not find princes," Cécile says. "Princesses find them."

Georges is very angry at Sebastian Sterling and all of his having-to-go business. He is very angry that his princess has no prince. But Georges still loves Polina. The best part of his day is when she comes outside, sits down on one of the docks along the canal, and has her coffee.

When Polina does that, even when she is sad, Georges thinks it is a very fine thing indeed to be a French duck.

The next afternoon, Polina does not come out and have her coffee on the edge of the canal. Instead, from inside of Polina's house, a silence spreads out across the canal. It is the sort of silence often called a hush. A hush is a silence you can see, and our French ducks know that it is most often seen in churches, or libraries, or concert halls. Or even in bedrooms. But it is rarely seen spreading out across canals.

And yet here it is in Venice—a hush coming from inside the room where Polina Panova makes her magical dresses. Georges and Cécile can see that this particular hush has a light. A golden light, with shining pink bits and bouncing blues woven into it. This light and this

hush make everyone who sees it and hears it happy and peaceful and amazed.

Even the mallards, at the other end of the canal, stop their lazy bickering to look.

"What is she doing in there?" Georges asks his sister. "When will she come out and have her coffee with us?"

But Cécile does not answer. She is looking at the light and listening to its hush. She is happy and peaceful and amazed.

The light can be seen all night and all the next day. And the next, and the next.

And then the light vanishes, along with the hush, and all the normal sounds of the canal return. If you listen, you do not hear the hush. Instead you hear the water moving, the green things growing, and the wind kissing everyone it meets.

No one sees Polina for a week.

"This will *not do*," Georges says. "Maybe we should peek through the windows and look for her."

"Wait," says Cécile. "Wait."

She is not sure what they should wait for, but she is sure that spying through Polina's windows is a very bad idea.

A day passes, and then another.

"I think we should peek through the windows," Georges says.

He and Cécile have finished their morning dive for the greenest, gunkiest breakfast they can find.

"I think you are right," Cécile says, and just then, right that second, the front door of Polina Panova's house opens.

"Hello," she says. "How are my favorite ducks?"

"Where have you been?" Georges asks. "Where did that light go? The gold one with the pink and blue in it?"

"Why did the hush stop?" Cécile asks.

She is very happy to see Polina, and glad that they will not have to spy through the windows.

"I have been working," Polina says. "The hush stopped because I found a way to put it into my dresses."

"Your dresses?" Georges asks.

"Yes," Polina says.

"You use thread, silk, cotton, and velvet to make your dresses," Georges says, in case she has forgotten.

"Also grass, flowers, pieces of the night sky, and strawberry jam," Cécile reminds him.

"And now I use that golden light Georges gave me," Polina says. "I had put it away in a drawer, because I did not know what to do with it."

"But now you do know," Cécile says. "Now you have that light and that hush in your dresses."

"Yes, and these dresses are unlike anything else I have made," Polina says proudly. "When you look at them, it is like hearing the snow fall."

The ducks are quiet, pondering how magical these dresses will be.

Suddenly Cécile says to Polina, "You aren't sad anymore."

"You aren't?" Georges asks.

"No, not as much as before," Polina says.

"Does that mean you are happy again?" Georges asks.

"She is happy about the dresses," Cécile says.

"Yes," Polina says. "That's right."

"You still seem a little bit sad," Georges says.

"I will always be a little sad that Sebastian Sterling had to go," Polina says.

"Always?" Georges asks, spreading out his wings to indicate displeasure. "Always be a little bit sad?"

"Yes," Polina says. "But I will be happy too. And I will make dresses."

"There will be so many people who want these dresses," Cécile says.

"So many!" Polina says happily, and goes back inside.

Back in the water, Georges is quiet a moment. He is thinking.

He swims down to where the mallards are slowly waking up.

"You are mallards," he says. "You have green necks and brown feathers."

The drakes, who have green necks, and the hens, who have brown feathers, look at him.

"Yes," they say. "We do."

Georges swims back to where his sister is.

"You are a French duck," he says. "You have glossy black feathers, a white tail, a long neck, and a yellow beak."

"Yes," Cécile says. "I do."

"Polina Panova is a Russian princess," Georges says. "How is it possible that she will always be sad?"

"A little bit sad," Cécile says.

"Princesses are not sad," Georges says. "Not even a little bit."

"And ducks who live in Venice are not French," Cécile says.

"But we are French," Georges says.

"And we live in Venice," says Cécile.

Georges looks at the mallards. He looks at Polina's sweet bungalow, where she makes dresses with the help of a golden, soothing light from where the ocean meets the sky. He knows that the next time he is hungry, there will be plenty of green gunky things to eat.

Georges wonders if Polina will ever look for a new prince. He wonders if a new prince will make cakes instead of movies. There might never be a new prince, or there might be one who will do nothing but kill dragons.

On the canal, in Venice, it is all possible.

"I like how it is," Georges says.

"Even with the silver shadows and shimmering light?" asks Cécile.

Georges thinks about how his eyes almost hurt when he was flying through the clouds made from silver shadows and shimmering light.

"Yes," he says. "Even with those."